MAGIC TREE HOUSE® #46
A MERLIN MISSION

Dogs in the Dead of Night

by Mary Pope Osborne

illustrated by Sal Murdocca

A STEPPING STONE BOOK™

Random House 🏠 New York

Text copyright © 2011 by Mary Pope Osborne
Jacket art and interior illustrations copyright © 2011 by Sal Murdocca

All rights reserved. Published in the United States by Random House Children's Books, a division of Random House, Inc., New York.

Random House and the colophon are registered trademarks and A Stepping Stone Book and the colophon are trademarks of Random House, Inc. Magic Tree House is a registered trademark of Mary Pope Osborne; used under license.

Visit us on the Web!
MagicTreeHouse.com
www.randomhouse.com/kids

Educators and librarians, for a variety of teaching tools, visit us at
www.randomhouse.com/teachers

Library of Congress Cataloging-in-Publication Data
Osborne, Mary Pope.
Dogs in the dead of night / by Mary Pope Osborne ; cover art and interior illustrations by Sal Murdocca. — 1st ed.
  p. cm. — (Magic tree house ; #46)
Summary: Jack and Annie travel to a monastery in the Swiss Alps where, with the help of St. Bernard dogs and magic, they seek the second of four special objects necessary to break the spell on the wizard Merlin's beloved penguin, Penny.
ISBN 978-0-375-86824-5 (trade) — ISBN 978-0-375-96824-2 (lib. bdg.) — ISBN 978-0-375-89876-1 (ebook)
[1. Magic—Fiction. 2. Time travel—Fiction. 3. Saint Bernard dog—Fiction. 4. Dogs—Fiction. 5. Brothers and sisters—Fiction. 6. Alps, Swiss (Switzerland)—History—19th century—Fiction. 7. Switzerland—History—1789–1815—Fiction.]
I. Murdocca, Sal, ill. II. Title.
PZ7.O81167Dn 2011 [Fic]—dc22 2010047554

Printed in the United States of America

10 9 8 7 6 5 4 3 2 1

Random House Children's Books supports the First Amendment and celebrates the right to read.

For Joey, Mr. Bezo, and Little Bear,
and in memory of Teddy and Bailey

And with special thanks to Janet Marlow
and Cheryl Barber and the Brushy Creek Saints

CONTENTS

*"His name is not Wild Dog anymore,
but the First Friend, because he will be our
friend for always and always and always."*
—from *Just So Stories* by Rudyard Kipling

PROLOGUE

One summer day in Frog Creek, Pennsylvania, a mysterious tree house appeared in the woods. It was filled with books. A boy named Jack and his sister, Annie, soon discovered that the tree house was magic, and just by pointing at a book, they could go to any time and any place in history. While they were gone, no time at all passed back in Frog Creek.

Jack and Annie eventually found out that the tree house belonged to Morgan le Fay, a magical librarian from the legendary realm of Camelot. They have since traveled on many adventures in the magic tree house and have completed many missions for both Morgan le Fay and Merlin the magician. On these journeys, they often received the help of two young enchanters from Camelot named Teddy and Kathleen.

Now Teddy and Kathleen are in desperate

need of Jack and Annie's help. While Merlin and Morgan were away, Teddy accidentally put a spell on Penny, Merlin's beloved penguin, and turned her into a stone statue. Teddy fears that he could be banished from the kingdom unless Jack and Annie can save Penny.

Teddy and Kathleen have found an ancient spell that will undo the one that Penny is under. To make the spell work, Jack and Annie must go on four adventures to collect four special things. They have just returned from a magic tree house journey to India, where they found the first thing: an emerald in the shape of a rose.

Now they are waiting for Teddy and Kathleen to send word about what they must find next. . . .

CHAPTER ONE

The Second Thing

"Jack, Jack!" whispered Annie.

Jack opened his eyes. He'd been dreaming about running away from cobras. "What's wrong?" he said, sitting up in bed. It was still dark outside.

"Nothing's wrong," whispered Annie. "We have to go to the tree house and come back before it's time to get ready for school."

"The tree house?" said Jack sleepily.

"Teddy and Kathleen may have translated the next lines of the spell," said Annie. "We have to see if they're there, or if they've sent a message."

"Huh?" said Jack. He was still half-asleep.

"We have to find the *second* thing to break the spell that turned Penny to stone!" said Annie. "Remember? Come on, Jack, wake up!" She shook his shoulder.

"Okay, okay. We have to get the second thing!" Jack jumped out of bed. "I'm ready!"

"No, you're not," said Annie. "You have to put your clothes on. I'll meet you downstairs."

Annie left the room, and Jack quickly changed out of his pajamas and into jeans and a sweat-shirt. He picked up his backpack and reached into an inside pocket. He pulled out the emerald rose they'd found in India. It was the first thing Teddy and Kathleen needed to break the spell and bring Penny back to life.

Jack grabbed his notebook and a pencil from his desk. He put them into his backpack along with the emerald rose. Then he slipped quietly out of his bedroom and down the stairs.

Annie was waiting on the front porch. The sky

was just starting to become light. The spring air was damp and cool. Jack was glad that he had worn his sweatshirt.

"All set," said Jack. "Let's go."

Jack and Annie ran across the wet grass of their front yard and dashed down the sidewalk. The houses they passed were all quiet, but the world of nature was awake with birdsong and dogs barking in the distance.

Jack and Annie crossed the street and headed into the Frog Creek woods. It was hard to see in the shadowy dark, but they were so familiar with the path to the tallest oak that they quickly found their way.

The tree house was there, waiting for them. But no one was looking out the window.

"Darn, no Teddy and Kathleen," said Annie.

"Well, at least they sent the tree house," said Jack. "That must mean they were able to translate the next part of the ancient spell. They must have stayed in Camelot to work on the rest."

"Yeah, probably," said Annie. She grabbed the rope ladder and started up. Jack followed her.

Inside the tree house, daylight was starting to creep through the windows. Jack saw a small scroll on top of a book in the shadows. "That's it!" he said. He picked it up and read aloud:

The second thing to break the spell
is a white and yellow flower.
Live its meaning for yourself,
if only for an hour.

"A white and yellow flower?" said Annie. "Well, that sounds easier than finding an emerald shaped like a rose."

"Okay. But where do we go to look for it?" said Jack. He picked up the book from the floor and read the title aloud:

THE SWISS ALPS

"What's that mean?" asked Annie. "The Swiss Alps?"

"Those are mountains in the country of Switzerland," said Jack. "People ski there and stuff. The Alps are the mountains they climb in *The Sound of Music.*"

"Oh, *that* place!" said Annie. "Great!"

"Look, there's a bookmark," said Jack. He turned to a page marked with a blue velvet ribbon. There was a picture of tall mountain peaks and an open, snowy area surrounded by rocky slopes. The caption read: *The Great Saint Bernard Pass.*

"That must be the exact place we're supposed to go," said Jack. "Ready?"

"Hold on—there's something else," said Annie. She picked up a small blue bottle from the floor of the shadowy corner. The bottle had a label on it. She read aloud:

One sip with a wish will turn you into anything you want for one hour. Use only once.

—Teddy and Kathleen

"Whoa," said Jack.

"*Anything* we want?" said Annie.

"That's what it says," said Jack.

"This is going to be so much fun!" said Annie. "Let's get going."

Annie handed Jack the bottle. He carefully put it and the scroll into his backpack. Then he pointed at the picture of the Great Saint Bernard Pass in their Alps book. "I wish we could go there!" he said.

The wind started to blow.

The tree house started to spin.

It spun faster and faster.

Then everything was still.

Absolutely still.

CHAPTER TWO

Buried Alive!

A cold wind swept through the window. The purple light of the setting sun filled the tree house. Jack and Annie wore scratchy wool pants, shirts, hats, scarves, and gloves, and leather shoes. Jack's pack had turned into a leather bag. When he opened it, he saw the scroll and the blue bottle inside—along with his notebook and pencil and the emerald rose.

"So these are the Swiss Alps," said Annie, shivering and looking out the window. "Pretty, but cold."

Jack looked out with her. The tree house was

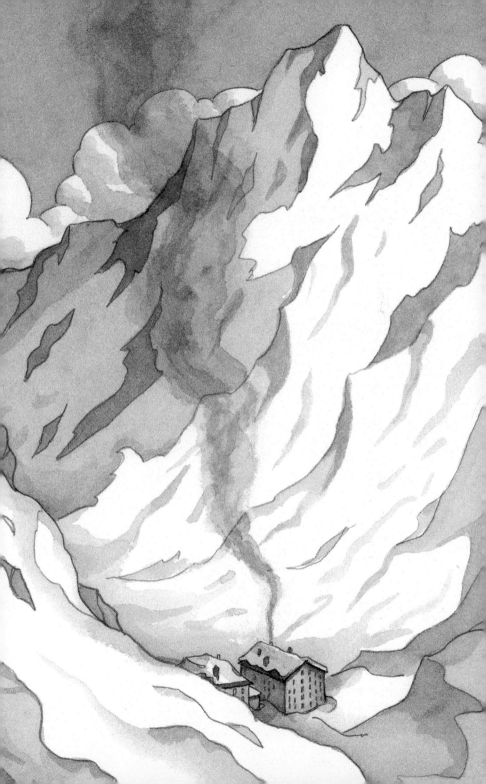

nestled between gray boulders on a mountain slope. Snowy peaks loomed overhead. Below the peaks was the snow-covered pass they had seen in the picture. Smoke rose from a tall building.

"This must be the Great Saint Bernard Pass," said Jack. He picked up their book and turned to the page with the bookmark and read:

> **The Great Saint Bernard Pass is an ancient road between the two highest peaks of the Alps. For thousands of years, it was the only route between Switzerland and Italy. The pass was named for Bernard of Menthon, who built a monastery there in the eleventh century. For hundreds of years, the monks at this Swiss monastery have welcomed cold and weary travelers who are crossing the pass.**

"So that building must be the monastery," said Jack.

"Great," said Annie. "We can start our mission by going there."

"Okay," said Jack. "But I don't get it. To save Penny we have to find a white and yellow flower. And we have to live its meaning, if only for an hour—whatever that means."

"We'll figure it out," said Annie.

"Let's hope," said Jack. "But where do we find flowers *here*?"

Jack and Annie looked out at the treeless landscape of ice, snow, and rock. "Well, there must be flowers *somewhere*," said Annie.

"I don't know," said Jack. "Maybe Teddy and Kathleen made a mistake and sent us to the wrong place."

"They've never made a mistake before," said Annie.

"Uh, excuse me. Teddy didn't make a mistake turning Penny into stone?" said Jack.

"Okay, good point," said Annie. "But let's head to the monastery before it gets dark. We can ask about flowers there."

"But what if—" started Jack.

"Stop worrying," interrupted Annie. "Our book says the monks welcome cold, weary travelers. I'm cold, and your questions are making me weary. Come on." She climbed out the window into the snow.

"Funny," said Jack. But he was ready to find shelter, too. His face was freezing. He packed up their book and slung the leather bag over his shoulder, then followed Annie out the tree house window.

Jack's feet crunched down onto the icy snow. As the sun went down behind the peaks, deep purple shadows climbed over the tall mountains. The monastery in the hollow below was completely hidden in darkness.

"We have to hurry," said Annie.

"No, we have to move *slowly* down the slope, so we don't slide," said Jack.

"Well, then let's move slowly *quickly*," said Annie.

Jack and Annie started down the slope. As they carefully put one foot in front of the other, a strange sound came from above: *whumph!*

"What was that?" said Jack, looking around.

Next came a low rumble like thunder.

"What's *that*?" said Annie.

Then came a noise like the sound of glass breaking.

"Whoa!" cried Jack.

Directly above them on the mountain, big blocks of snow were breaking into smaller chunks and sliding down the slope.

"Grab my hand!" shouted Jack. He reached for Annie, and she gripped his hand.

Suddenly snow was moving all around them! Even the snow beneath them was sliding! A block of icy snow slammed into Jack, knocking him away from Annie.

"Jack!" Annie cried.

Another chunk of snow knocked Jack off his feet and sent him tumbling headfirst down the slope. Jack kept falling downhill until a wall of frozen snow stopped him. He tried to stand, but a giant wave of soft, powdery snow blew over him, burying him completely.

Jack kicked his arms and legs, trying to surface from the fluffy sea of snow. He kicked and flailed, but the harder he struggled, the more snow there seemed to be. Snow clogged Jack's eyes, ears, and throat. Every time he coughed, he sucked in more snow. He felt as if he were drowning—until he finally pushed his head up through the snow into the cold air.

He could breathe!

But Jack still couldn't see. A gust of snow powder blinded him. He couldn't move his arms or hands, his legs or feet. The soft snow around his body had turned hard and solid. Jack felt as if he were trapped in cold concrete, buried up to his neck. Where was Annie? Had she been buried alive, too?

Jack tried to yell, but no sound came from his

throat. He kept trying to shout for Annie, but it was hopeless. His lips wouldn't move. He couldn't even feel his mouth. He couldn't feel his arms or legs, feet or hands. He closed his eyes. He couldn't feel anything, not even the wind that kept blowing snow in his face. . . .

❄ ❄ ❄

Owww! Jack screamed in his head. His eyes shot open. He was freezing cold, and creatures were attacking him! They were whimpering, snuffling, panting, whining. *Wild dogs!* Jack thought with terror.

Two dogs were scratching and digging all around Jack's body. A third dog licked his eyes and ears and the top of his head! Jack felt as if he were about to be licked to death!

Help! Jack tried to shout. But no sound came from his clogged throat. *Help! Help!* His mind roared. But the three huge, panting creatures kept licking him and pawing the icy snow that had trapped Jack's body.

As the giant dogs hovered over him, Jack saw flames behind them. Figures in hooded robes were moving about in the fiery light, carrying torches. The figures were scarier than the dogs.

"Jack!" came a faint cry.

"Annie?" Jack croaked.

A man shouted, and the dogs backed off. The flaming torches shone directly on Jack. He could see that he'd been mostly dug out of the snow, but he still couldn't feel or move his body.

Two of the hooded figures leaned down and tightly gripped Jack's arms. They pulled him to his feet. When they let go of him, he started to fall. They grabbed him again and lifted him onto a cloth stretcher.

"My—my sister . . . ," Jack chattered. He managed to lift his head and look back. In the torchlight, he saw Annie lying on a stretcher, wrapped in a blanket.

"She is safe," said one of the men.

"Who—who are you?" Jack asked, shivering uncontrollably. He had lost his hat and scarf in the snow.

"We are monks from the Saint Bernard Monastery," the man answered. He covered Jack with a heavy blanket.

"Oh . . . thank you," whispered Jack.

The three dogs led the way over the snowy pass, snorting and sneezing and panting. The monks followed, carrying Jack and Annie through the cold, windy dark.

CHAPTER THREE

The Saints

When they reached the monastery, the monks lowered the two stretchers to the ground. They helped Jack and Annie to their feet and then led them up a short flight of steps to a big wooden door.

"You okay?" Jack asked Annie.

"Yes," she said. "You?"

"Just cold," Jack said, shivering.

One monk rang a large bell outside the door. Another handed Jack his leather bag. "We found this beside you," the man said.

"Oh, thanks," said Jack. He'd forgotten all about the bag.

Someone inside pulled open the door. Jack and Annie limped into a torchlit hallway with a vaulted ceiling and a wide staircase. The monks and three dogs followed.

The monks lifted their hoods, revealing friendly faces. For the first time, Jack got a good look at the huge, panting dogs. They were Saint Bernards with white and reddish-brown fur. They had powerful heads, square muzzles, and drooping jowls.

As the monks who had rescued Jack and Annie went down the hall with the dogs, two other monks stepped forward. They both wore dark robes and round black caps.

"Welcome," one said in a deep, warm voice. He was a large man with a rugged face. "I am Father Laurent, the head of the monastery."

"And I am Brother Michael," said the other monk. He was not much taller than Jack, and his face was smooth and rosy.

"We're Jack and Annie," Jack said hoarsely. He still didn't have his full voice.

"Thanks for saving us," said Annie.

"We were happy to do so," said Father Laurent. "You must come and sit by the fire in the parlor to warm yourselves and dry your clothes. Brother Michael will take you there while I ask our cook to warm some soup for you."

"Thanks," said Annie. "That sounds great."

Jack nodded. He wanted to lie down, but at the same time he was hungry and cold.

"Come with me," said Brother Michael. "Are you able to walk on your own?"

"Sure," said Jack.

Jack and Annie could walk without help, but they both limped a little as they followed Brother Michael down the hall into the dimly lit parlor. The three Saint Bernards were resting in front of a huge fireplace. "Wow," breathed Annie. The dogs barely looked up.

"Please, sit by the fire," said Brother Michael.

Jack and Annie sat on wooden chairs and stared in a daze at the crackling fire. A moment later, Father Laurent came into the room and handed them bowls of steaming soup. The two monks waited as Jack and Annie drank the hot broth.

By the time they had emptied their bowls, Jack was feeling much better. The hot liquid had warmed his insides, and the heat from the fire had nearly dried his clothes.

"Thank you. I feel a lot better now," Annie said to the two monks.

"You must stay here and rest for the night," said Father Laurent. "You can continue your journey in the morning when you are rested."

"Thank you," said Jack.

The monk looked at them curiously. "You must be very brave to try to travel the pass in the dark," he said.

"Or not very smart," Annie said.

Father Laurent smiled. "Yes, but I did not want to say that," he said.

"No kidding; we were looking for flowers!" said Annie.

"Goodness," said Brother Michael. "I am afraid you've come to the wrong place to pick flowers."

Both monks chuckled, and Annie laughed with them. Jack could barely smile—he was worried. *I knew we came to the wrong place!* he thought.

"Now tell me, why were you really traveling on the pass?" asked Father Laurent.

"Well . . . um . . . actually, we're on a mission," said Jack.

"Indeed?" said Brother Michael.

"Yes . . . we . . . um . . . ," Jack said.

"We're on a mission to learn more about the Alps," said Annie.

"That's right," said Jack. "We're doing a report."

"But you are very young," said Brother Michael.

"We *are* young," said Annie. "But we are serious researchers. In fact, we recently went to India and studied the Taj Mahal. It's amazingly beautiful. Have you ever seen it?"

"Uh, no, we haven't," said Brother Michael.

He seemed a little surprised, but Father Laurent only smiled.

Before either monk could say any more, Annie continued, "I have some questions right now about these mountain dogs. Jack, get out your notebook."

Jack reached into his bag and took out his pencil and notebook.

"So," Annie said in a serious voice, "exactly how did your dogs know that we needed help?"

"Well, the Saints always know if someone is trapped in the snow," said Brother Michael.

"The Saints?" asked Jack.

The monk pointed to the dogs lying near the hearth. "Our Saint Bernard dogs," he said. "We have fifteen of them. We call them simply the Saints. They were named after Saint Bernard, who founded the monastery."

"Oh, right," said Jack. "Saint Bernard of Menthon." He pushed his glasses back and took notes:

"Saints" are rescue dogs

"The Saints have saved over a thousand people from the White Death," said Brother Michael.

"And the White Death is . . . what?" Jack asked, looking up.

"That is what we call blizzards and avalanches," said Brother Michael. "You were directly in the path of a very small avalanche. They are quite common in the spring. When the snow begins to melt, it loses its grip on the mountainside and slides down."

Jack wrote:

Avalanches:
Often in spring
Snow melts and slides
Called White Death

"You were lucky," said Father Laurent. "Avalanche victims rarely survive if they are trapped for long in the snow. Even a very small avalanche can be deadly."

"So there wasn't much time for the Saints to find us and save us, was there?" said Annie.

"No," said Father Laurent. "But they need no compass. Once they hear the voice of the snow, as we call it, their noses lead them in the right direction. They can find their way to a person buried six feet down."

"Oh, man," Jack murmured, and wrote:

Saint Bernards:
Hear "voice of snow"
Great noses

"Wow, they're amazing," said Annie. Everyone looked at the dogs. "Thank you, Saints, for saving our lives," Annie said to them.

The gentle giants didn't seem to care about being heroes. One scratched his ear, another yawned, and the third one snored.

Father Laurent laughed at the dogs. "Well,

Jack and Annie. I imagine you would like to sleep now," he said.

Jack closed his notebook and nodded.

"We're pretty tired," said Annie.

"Come. I will take you to your room," Brother Michael said.

"Good night, Jack and Annie," said Father Laurent. "And farewell, for I will not be seeing you in the morning. I am setting out first thing to help the French army."

What does that mean? wondered Jack.

"Thanks for everything," said Annie.

"Of course," said Father Laurent. "I am glad you are safe now. No one should ever be caught on these mountains in the dead of night."

CHAPTER FOUR

Barry

Jack and Annie followed Brother Michael out of the parlor. The monk carried two lanterns and chatted while he led them down a chilly hall.

"This monastery was built on the highest part of the pass almost eight hundred years ago," Brother Michael said. "We have a dog kennel and a chapel, as well as a library filled with books and exhibits of rocks, minerals, and butterflies. Father Laurent is quite well known for his research and his nature expeditions."

"That's cool," murmured Jack. But he was too worried about their mission to say any more. *How will we ever find a flower here?* he wondered again.

Brother Michael opened a door to a small room. "We have many rooms for travelers," he said. "But tonight you are our only visitors."

The monk placed a lantern on a table between two small beds. "I hope you will sleep well," he said. "And if you have more questions, I will be glad to answer them tomorrow."

"Thanks. Good night," said Annie.

"Good night," said Brother Michael, and he left the room and closed the door.

Jack and Annie sat on their beds. The lantern light was casting shadows on the white walls of the small room. The wind rattled the windowpanes.

"I'm so glad to be *here*," Annie said, sighing, "and not lost outside in the dead of night." She lay back and covered herself with a brown woolen blanket.

"No kidding," said Jack. "But it still makes no

sense that Teddy and Kathleen sent us here."

"We'll figure it out tomorrow," said Annie.

Jack reached into his bag and took out the small scroll. He unrolled it and read aloud by the lantern light:

The second thing to break the spell
is a white and yellow flower.
Live its meaning for yourself,
if only for an hour.

"It's a mystery," said Jack. "No flower can live in a cold, snowy place like this. And live its meaning? What's that about? And why just an hour?"

"I don't know," murmured Annie. She closed her eyes and yawned. "Aren't you tired?"

"Yeah, very," said Jack. "But I'm also worried about our mission." He put the scroll back into his bag and pulled out their research book.

Jack flipped through it until he came to a section with photos of plants and animals. He read the chapter title aloud: "Flora and Fauna of the

Alps." He looked at Annie. "*Flora* and *fauna*
means *plants* and *animals*. Did you know that?"

Annie didn't open her eyes or say anything.

"Are you asleep?" asked Jack.

"Yes," said Annie. "You should go to sleep, too.
You can read all this stuff in the morning."

"But nothing makes sense," said Jack. "I don't
know if I *can* sleep."

"Try," said Annie.

Jack sighed. He closed the research book and
placed it on the floor. Then he blew out the lantern
flame and pulled up his wool blanket.

Jack kept his eyes open, but he couldn't see
a thing. The room was pitch-black. From somewhere in the monastery came soft, beautiful singing. Two or three Saints barked. The panes of
their window rattled as the wind moaned outside.

"We forgot to ask what year it is," said Jack.
"It's hard to tell, don't you think?"

"Shhh," whispered Annie.

"But it feels timeless here," Jack went on.
"Everything could be in a time long ago or in our

time: sun, snow, mountains, monks, soup, singing . . . wind . . . wool . . . night . . ." Jack closed his eyes.

"And dogs . . . ," murmured Annie.

"Dogs . . . ," Jack repeated in a whisper.

And he fell asleep.

❊ ❊ ❊

Jack opened his eyes. Cold gray light came through a paned window. *Where am I?* he wondered. He sat up, put his glasses on, and looked around the white-walled room. Annie was still asleep.

Oh, yeah, the monastery, Jack thought. "Hey, Annie," he whispered. "Wake up."

"Where are we?" Annie asked, opening her eyes.

"In the Swiss Alps," said Jack.

"We are? Why?" Annie asked groggily.

"Good question," said Jack. "Let's read about flora and fauna of the Alps and figure it out."

Jack reached for the book on the floor. Just as he grabbed it, the door banged open, and a Saint Bernard dog burst into the room. The dog flung himself onto Jack's bed.

"Ahhh!" Jack yelled.

"Whoa!" cried Annie.

The giant dog plopped down on top of Jack and panted, *HEH-HEH-HEH!* His head was as big as a basketball. His breath smelled like fish and crackers. His fur smelled like wet wool.

"Okay, get off, please!" said Jack. He tried to push the dog off, but the dog just wrinkled his brow and looked curiously into Jack's eyes. Drool hung from his long jowls.

"Eww! Annie, help!" said Jack.

"Hey, *you*!" Annie called to the huge, panting dog. "Come to *me*!"

The Saint Bernard jumped off Jack and bounded onto Annie's bed with the same joy and energy. Annie couldn't stop giggling as the dog licked her face.

"Barry!" said Brother Michael. He stood in the doorway.

Ignoring the monk, the dog nuzzled Annie with his giant head. "Stop! Stop!" she said, laughing.

"Barry! Off!" the monk said.

"Barry!" said Jack, trying to help.

The dog looked over at Jack. Then he leapt off Annie's bed.

"Oh, no!" cried Jack. "Don't come back to me!" He covered his head with his blanket.

But it was too late. Barry jumped back onto Jack's bed and started pawing at the blanket, trying to dig Jack out from underneath.

"Barry, come!" commanded Brother Michael. "Now!"

Finally the Saint Bernard leapt off Jack's bed and bounded into the hallway.

Brother Michael quickly closed the door behind the rowdy giant. "Well! Now you've met Barry!" he said.

Out in the hallway, Barry whined and pawed at the door, begging to come back into the room.

"Oh, poor puppy," said Annie.

"Barry may be young," said Brother Michael. "But he is a two-hundred-pound dog who needs to grow up."

"Aww," said Annie. She laughed tenderly at the mournful sounds Barry was making.

"Perhaps you do not realize this," said Brother

Michael, "but it is past noon. You have both been asleep for many hours."

"Really? Oh, man!" said Jack. He jumped off the bed and grabbed his shoes and put them on. He couldn't believe they'd wasted so much time!

"We are just completing our noontime meal in the dining hall before we hike down the pass," said Brother Michael. "Thousands of French soldiers will be crossing soon on their way to Italy. Father Laurent left to assist the first troops. I thought perhaps you would like to eat something before the rest of us leave to help."

"Uh—sure, thanks," said Jack.

"I will wait for you in the dining hall next to the parlor," said the monk.

When Brother Michael slipped out the door, Barry greeted him with a happy yelp. Then the giant dog's barking faded down the hallway.

CHAPTER FIVE

He's All Yours

"Come on, hurry," said Annie, pulling on her shoes.

"But we have to look in our book," said Jack, "and try to figure out—"

"Let's look after we talk to Brother Michael," said Annie. "He's leaving soon. And I have a feeling that he—or someone else here—is going to help us."

"Let's hope," said Jack.

Still sore from the avalanche, Jack limped a

little as he followed Annie out of their room. They passed all the closed doors lining the long torch-lit hallway, until finally they came to the parlor. From the dining hall, they could hear the clinking of silverware and china, but no voices.

Jack and Annie peered into the room and saw about forty monks sitting on benches on either side of a long table. Brother Michael waved from one end. The other monks didn't even look up. They all kept their heads bowed as they silently finished eating their noontime meal.

Jack and Annie crossed the dining hall, weaving among a dozen Saint Bernards resting with their heads on their paws. None of them had Barry's crazy energy.

Jack and Annie sat at the end of a bench across from Brother Michael. One of the other monks served them bread and butter, bowls of porridge, and cups of hot tea.

Jack took a sip of the milky, sweet tea. Then he leaned across the table to Brother Michael.

"Excuse me," he whispered, "but is there another place in these mountains—a place not too far from here—where we might find flowers?"

Brother Michael looked thoughtful. Then he shook his head. "Certainly not now. It has been a very cold spring. But a month from now, at a lower altitude, you will definitely find flowers."

"Not until a month from now?" said Jack.

"I am afraid not," said Brother Michael. He smiled curiously at Jack. "You must love flowers very much."

Jack didn't know what to say. How could he possibly explain that they had to find a white and yellow flower and live its meaning for an hour to help break a spell to save Merlin's penguin, who'd been turned to stone by a young sorcerer in Camelot?

"Um . . . yes, I do like them," said Jack.

"Perhaps you could go on a climbing trip with Father Laurent if you come back this way in the summer," said Brother Michael. "He also loves plants and flowers and is an expert on the flora of the Alps."

Jack nodded. He picked up a chunk of bread and took a small bite. *That would be great,* he thought, *except we can't wait!* His only hope was that their research book could help them somehow.

By now, all the monks were getting up from the table. The Saints quietly followed them out of the dining hall. As Jack ate his bread and watched everyone leave, Barry bounded out of the kitchen.

He grabbed the last bite of bread right out of Jack's hand and gulped it down!

"Hey!" said Jack.

Annie burst out laughing. "Barry! You thief!" she cried.

Without a word, Brother Michael grabbed Barry by the collar. But the dog broke loose from the monk and ran around the room. He went down on his forelegs. He barked his happy, booming bark, as if daring them to catch him.

Annie laughed again.

Brother Michael sighed. "I apologize for the theft of your bread," he said to Jack. "May I get you some more?"

"No, no, it's okay," said Jack.

Barry's barks shook the dining hall.

"Excuse me, I will take him to the kitchen," Brother Michael said. He grabbed Barry by the collar again. This time he held on tight and pulled him into the kitchen.

The dining hall was empty now, except for Jack and Annie. "Listen, we can't waste any more time," said Jack, rising from the table. "I'm going back to our room to read about flora and fauna of the Alps."

"I'll go with you," said Annie.

As Jack and Annie were leaving, Brother Michael came out of the kitchen alone. "I apologize for Barry," he said, frowning. "He will be leaving us tomorrow."

"Why? Where's he going?" asked Annie.

"Down to a house in the valley," said the monk.

"But he seems so happy here," said Annie.

"Oh, he is *very* happy here," said Brother Michael. "Too happy. It will break his heart to leave."

"So why does he have to leave?" said Annie.

"Because he has a very independent spirit, and none of us has the time to give him the extra training he needs," said Brother Michael.

"Well, what if *I* try to train him?" said Annie.

"What?" Jack looked at her in surprise.

"No, really. I can do it," Annie said. She turned back to the monk. "You can give that job to me. I know about training dogs. And I'm really good with animals. Right, Jack?"

"Yeah, but—" said Jack.

"Please, let me try," Annie said to Brother Michael.

"You are very kind. However—" Brother Michael was interrupted by howling from the kitchen. The monk shook his head. "Listen to him! He will cry night and day if he has to leave us. And Father Laurent shall miss him terribly. . . ." He paused and looked at Annie. "Perhaps we should give him one more chance, if you really think you can handle him. Shall I put him in your charge today, and we will see what training you can give him?"

"Yes!" said Annie.

"Good. Then I will bring him to you," said Brother Michael, and he headed back to the kitchen.

"Are you nuts?" Jack whispered to Annie. "You don't know how to train a crazy dog like that."

"Actually, I *do*," said Annie. "For your information, I just read a book on training dogs. I even wrote a book report about it."

"But you haven't had any practice," said Jack. "And even if you had, we don't have time now. What about saving Penny? Did you forget our mission?"

"No. I was thinking this would give us an excuse to stay here longer," said Annie.

"Yeah . . . okay," said Jack. "But stay for *what*? Brother Michael said there are no flowers around here now. We'd have to stay for a month."

"Okay, okay," said Annie. "Listen, what about the magic potion? We can change into anything we want for an hour."

"Yeah. So . . . ?" said Jack.

"Well . . . do you think we could wish to change into something like . . . like official finders of white and yellow flowers?" asked Annie.

"No, that's—" said Jack.

"Stupid, yeah," said Annie. "So let's think."

Before they had time to think, Brother Michael came out of the kitchen. He was carrying monks' robes and had Barry on a leash.

The huge dog dragged Brother Michael over to Jack and Annie, swinging his tail and barking with excitement.

"You can work with him in the enclosed yard," said Brother Michael. He pointed to a door off the dining hall. "And you may want to wear these over your clothes, as it's quite cold outside." He handed them the monks' robes.

Jack and Annie pulled on the robes and tied the rope belts around their waists. Then they lifted their hoods over their heads.

"Perfect!" said Annie. "Much warmer!"

"Good," said Brother Michael. "He's all yours!" He handed Barry's leash to Jack. Jack gripped it with both hands as the big dog tugged on the other end.

"All of us will be gone from the monastery for the afternoon," said Brother Michael. "If you take a walk, you must not let Barry off the leash. Whatever you do, do not let him run freely outside. I am certain he would dash off to explore the mountains and get lost in the snow."

"Don't worry. We'll keep him in the yard," said Annie.

"I am very grateful for your help," said Brother Michael. "Perhaps this will even assist you with your research about the Alps."

"I'll bet it will," said Annie. "Well, good-bye. Good luck!"

Brother Michael smiled. "I fear *you* are the ones who will need luck today," he said. "Be good, Barry." Then the rosy-faced monk hurried off to catch up with the others.

"Okay! Let's get started!" said Annie. "Come on, Barry!" She threw open the door to a snowy yard surrounded by a rock wall.

Barry instantly lurched toward the yard.

"Arrgh!" cried Jack as the dog nearly yanked his arms off.

CHAPTER SIX

Good Dog?

Barry dragged Jack out the door of the dining hall into the yard. The air was cold and damp. The sky was gray, and the mountain peaks were shrouded in mist.

"Barry, sit!" said Annie.

But Barry didn't sit. Instead, he put his nose to the ground and pulled Jack all around the yard. He smelled the snow and the rock walls. Then he raised his head and closed his eyes, sniffing the air.

What does he smell? Jack wondered. Jack

couldn't smell anything in the cold mountain air.

Annie ran to Jack and Barry and scratched Barry behind his ear. "Come on, Barry! Let's get to work!" she said with enthusiasm.

The big dog opened his eyes and wagged his tail. His whole body seemed to be wagging.

"Now, Barry, to start with, you have to learn three commands," Annie said. "*Come, sit,* and *stay.*"

Barry sneezed as if to say, *No problem!*

Annie turned to Jack. "When he obeys a command, we give him lots of praise. We should act really positive and upbeat. That's what my book said."

Jack rolled his eyes.

"Positive," Annie repeated. "Upbeat. Let's start with *come.* I'll hold him. You walk away and then stop and say, '*Come, Barry!*'"

Jack sighed and handed Annie the leash. She struggled to keep Barry with her as Jack walked about twenty feet away. Jack turned and said,

"Come, Barry!" Annie let go of the leash. Barry charged toward Jack. When he reached him, he jumped up and put his paws on Jack's shoulders. Jack fell backward into the snow.

"Oww!" said Jack.

"Good dog!" Annie said, clapping.

Barry leaned over and slurped his tongue across Jack's face and ears.

"Yuck! Stop, stop!" said Jack. He scrambled to his feet before Barry could give him more sloppy kisses.

Annie ran over and patted Barry as she repeated, "Good dog, good dog."

Barry's eyes were bright and happy. He panted with short quick breaths, as if he were laughing.

"*Good* dog?" said Jack. "You've got to be kidding."

"Yes! He did what you said! You said '*come*,' and he came!" said Annie. "Come on, Jack. Positive! Upbeat!"

"Oh, sorry," said Jack, wiping his ears with his sleeve. "I love your slobber, Barry. It's my favorite thing."

"Okay, say that all over again, but use a happy voice," said Annie.

"Don't be ridiculous," said Jack. "Come on, let's move along."

"Right," said Annie. "I think he's got *come*. Here, take the leash back, and we'll do *sit*. Ready, Barry? *Sit!*"

Annie pushed down on Barry's rear end, and Barry sat. "Good dog!" Annie said. "Now pull the leash up, Jack, so he lifts his head."

Jack tugged on the leash, pulling Barry's head up. The Saint Bernard looked into Jack's eyes. Then he leapt up and licked Jack's face with his huge pink tongue. Jack yelped and fell backward again into the snow.

Before Barry could pounce on him, Jack scrambled to his feet, nearly tripping on his robe. "Oh, man!" he said to Barry. "What is wrong with you?"

"Nothing's wrong with him, Jack," said Annie. "He just likes you!"

"Well, tell him *not* to like me so much," said Jack.

"Come on, Jack. Be positive," Annie said.

"No. I'm done with training," said Jack. "You

can do it by yourself. I'm going inside to read about flora and fauna in our research book."

"But it's easier with two of us," said Annie. "Just one more command? Please?"

Annie looked hopefully at Jack. Barry looked at Jack, too. His tail had stopped wagging.

"Oh, okay," said Jack, sighing. "One more command."

"Yay, thanks!" said Annie.

Barry barked and wagged his tail.

"Let's try the *stay* command," said Annie. "We'll teach Barry to go down on all fours and stay—like all the dogs in the dining hall this morning."

"He'll never be that calm," said Jack.

Annie handed him the leash. "Here. Now try to gently pull Barry's head down while I press between his shoulder blades. See, I memorized all this stuff. Okay, Jack?"

"Yeah, yeah," Jack said. He knelt in front of Barry and gently pulled down on the leash.

Annie pushed Barry's shoulders with the palms of her hands. Barry didn't move. "I can't find his shoulder blades," said Annie. "Try this, Jack. Pull on his front legs. Pull them out in front of him."

Jack grabbed Barry's forelegs and pulled. Barry jumped up and put his paws on Jack's shoulders again, knocking him into the snow for the third time. Then the giant dog flopped onto Jack's chest, pinning him to the ground.

"Get off!" gasped Jack. "I can't breathe!" But Barry's brown eyes just stared happily at Jack. His cold, wet nose sniffed Jack's face. "Get-off-me-now-please!" commanded Jack.

Annie laughed. "You really love Jack, don't you, Barry?" she said.

Barry answered, *YES!* with a big sneeze right in Jack's face. Then he bounded to his feet.

"Eww, Jack!" said Annie, laughing.

"Gross!" cried Jack, wiping his face with the rough sleeve of his robe. "Okay, that's it." He scrambled to his feet. "I'm done. I'm *so* done with this. See you guys inside."

"Wait, we'll go with you," said Annie. "Come on, Barry. We'll do more training later. But you did a really great job! What a good dog!"

"Oh, brother," said Jack.

Barry sneezed again and gave his body a shake. Annie held the door, and the big dog trotted into the monastery, his head held high.

CHAPTER SEVEN

I Don't Believe It

Jack and Annie followed Barry inside. In the dining hall, Barry bounded over to one of the large dog bowls and slurped water. He splashed more outside of the bowl than he actually drank. When he finished, he galumphed toward Jack, water and drool flying out of his mouth.

"Stay away from me!" said Jack, pushing Barry away. "Annie, I'm going to go read now."

Jack hurried out of the dining hall and headed down the hallway toward their room. But Annie and Barry dashed ahead of him. The dog's playful barks echoed through the monastery, making it seem full of life, despite its emptiness.

As soon as they entered their bedroom, Jack closed the door and grabbed their book. Barry jumped onto Annie's bed. As Jack started to read about flora and fauna in the Alps, Barry yelped. He leapt up and barked at the door.

"What now?" said Jack.

"Someone's ringing the bell!" said Annie. "The bell at the front door. Hear it?"

Jack could barely hear the bell clanging over Barry's barking.

"We'd better go answer it," said Annie. "No one else is here. Come on, Barry."

"No, wait," said Jack. "I'll go with you. Barry should stay here, so he doesn't jump all over whoever's there."

"Okay, wait here, Barry," said Annie.

Jack left the book on his bed, and he and Annie hurried out of the room. Before Barry could follow them, Jack closed the door tightly. The dog howled.

"Don't cry! We'll be back soon!" shouted Annie. Then she and Jack hurried down the torchlit hallway to the front entrance.

The bell kept clanging.

Annie opened the heavy wooden door, and she and Jack peered out.

Two men in military uniforms stood on the steps of the monastery. One had a black mustache, and the other had bushy sideburns. Both wore blue and white coats with red cuffs and red collars. White pants were tucked into their riding boots. Swords hung from their sides.

Jack was startled. The soldiers looked as if they'd stepped out of a time long ago.

"Good afternoon. We think one of our officers may be here," said the soldier with the mustache.

"Um, I'm afraid your officer isn't here," said Annie. "No one's here but us. All the monks have left to help the French army."

"We are an advance party, and our officer got separated from us," said the second soldier. "Consul Napoléon hoped he had made his way here on his own."

"Napoléon?" asked Jack.

"First Consul Napoléon Bonaparte," the soldier said.

Oh, man, thought Jack. *Napoléon Bonaparte was a famous military leader of France!*

"When our officer arrives, please tell him to wait for us," said the man with the mustache. "We will return later." The two soldiers turned and walked away from the monastery.

Jack whirled around to Annie. "Did you hear the name of their leader? Napoléon Bonaparte! He lived two hundred years ago! Let's go look in our book! Maybe it has information about Napoléon crossing the Alps!"

Jack and Annie hurried down the torchlit hallway to their room. "Oh, wow," Jack said, pointing at one of the torches. "I should have figured out we weren't in *our* time! We don't use torches and lanterns for lighting anymore."

"Well, you've had a lot on your mind," said Annie.

"Monks seem timeless," Jack went on. "But as soon as you see a soldier, you can start to figure out the time in history. I can't wait to read about this in our book. Maybe there will be a clue to help us with our mission."

Jack ran the rest of the way to their room. He opened the door and stopped. "Oh, no," he said. "I ... don't ... believe ... it."

Annie caught up to Jack and peered into the room. "Oh, Barry," she said.

Barry was sitting on the floor, wagging his tail. Paper was hanging from his mouth.

"He *ate* our Alps book," said Jack, stunned. "He *ate* it!"

All around the room were bits and pieces of paper. Jack started collecting the pieces, but it was hopeless. Most of the book was in Barry's stomach. "I really don't believe this," said Jack.

"Bad dog, Barry!" yelled Annie.

Barry stopped wagging his tail. He lowered his head.

"Bad," said Annie sternly. "Bad, bad, bad!"

Barry kept his head low and wiggled his way toward the door. Then he stood up, and with his tail drooping, he slunk out of the room.

Jack flopped down on his bed and stared at the ceiling. "There's no hope now," he said. "We'll never read about flora and fauna in the Alps or about Napoléon or anything. I feel like we'll never figure out this mission or save Penny."

Annie sat next to him. "I'm sorry," she said.

"It's not your fault," said Jack.

"Well, I shouldn't have offered to train Barry," said Annie. "We should have studied the book when you wanted to."

Jack shook his head. "Whatever," he said. "I just don't know what to do next. We can't go home yet. We can't give up. We have to save Penny."

"I know, I know," said Annie. "Maybe we should just go outside and walk around. Get some fresh air. Want to?"

"I guess," said Jack. He picked up his bag and sighed. "Maybe if we just walk around, we'll think of something."

"Let's find Barry first," said Annie.

"Why?" said Jack. "So he can 'help' us some more?"

"No, I just want to make sure he's okay," said Annie. "I feel kind of bad for yelling."

Jack and Annie headed out of the room and down the hall.

"Barry!" Annie called.

There was no sign of him.

"I wonder where he went," Annie said. "Barry!"

"When he comes, just don't tell him he's a good dog," said Jack.

They passed the dining hall and looked inside. "Barry?" Annie called. But the room was empty.

Jack and Annie kept walking, until they got to the parlor. "Barry?" Annie called, peering in. But that room was empty, too.

Jack felt a cold wind blowing. It grew colder as he and Annie kept walking down the hallway, heading for the front door.

"Barry!" Annie called.

The whole monastery felt quiet and empty and

cold. Jack and Annie were both shivering by the time they reached the front hall.

"I wonder where— *Oh, no!*" said Annie. "Look!" She pointed to the front door. It was open. "We must not have closed the door hard enough and the wind blew it open! Barry must have gotten out!"

Annie rushed outside. "Barry! Barry!"

"Oh, man," said Jack. He hurried out into the cold, too. "Barry! Barry!"

The only sound they heard was the wind whistling over the pass. The only sight was snow flying through the air.

"He's run away!" wailed Annie. "I know it!"

"Barry!" Jack called.

"He'll get lost!" said Annie. "Brother Michael said he should never run loose—he'll get lost and never find his way home!"

"He couldn't have gone far," said Jack. "Don't panic. We'll find him."

Jack and Annie began wandering through the cold, shouting, "Barry! Barry!"

Gusts of wind blew over the pass, swirling the snow around them.

"Barry! Barry!" they called.

Jack kept expecting to see the big dog bounding through the white powder. How could he just disappear?

"I don't know what to do," Annie said, hugging herself. They both stopped walking. They were shivering in their robes, and their teeth chattered.

"Maybe we should go back and look through the monastery again," said Jack.

"No, I know he's not there!" said Annie. "I can feel it! He's lost somewhere, I'm sure of it!" Tears filled her eyes. "I really hurt his feelings when I said *bad, bad, bad*. He didn't know our book was so important. He thought he was a good dog. I kept telling him he was a good dog. But really he wasn't a very good dog, Jack. He was just a funny, happy dog! I should have closed the door all the way!" Tears ran down Annie's red cheeks. "I feel terrible."

"Hey, hey, it wasn't *your* fault," said Jack. "I

feel terrible, too. *I* could have closed the door. But don't worry. When the others come back, the dogs can help us find him."

"That's a long time from now," said Annie, still crying. "It'll be really dark."

"I know," said Jack. He put his hand on Annie's back and spoke gently. "But the Saints can find him in the dark, like they found us. If they can smell people really far away, they can smell a big dog like Barry."

"I wish *we* could smell him right now," said Annie. "I wish we were dogs. Then we could find him." She covered her face and sobbed.

"You wish we were dogs?" said Jack.

"Yes," said Annie, sniffling, "so we could find him."

"Well . . ." Jack took a deep breath. "Okay. I think I know what we can do," he said.

"What? What can we do?" asked Annie, wiping her face.

"*This* is what we can do," said Jack. He reached

into his bag and pulled out the tiny bottle from Teddy and Kathleen.

Annie stared at Jack. "Oh, wow!" she breathed.

"We can use *this* to turn into dogs and find Barry," said Jack.

"Jack! That's the best idea you've ever had!" said Annie.

Jack smiled. "Okay, here's what we'll do," he said. "We'll each take a sip. Then together, we'll say: *'Turn us into Saint Bernard dogs!'*"

"And we'll turn into dogs for an hour!" said Annie.

"Dogs for an hour," said Jack. He took another deep breath. Then he pulled the cork out of the bottle.

CHAPTER EIGHT

Dogs for an Hour

"Ready?" said Jack.

Annie nodded. "Ready," she said.

Jack took a sip of the potion and handed the bottle to Annie. She took a sip and put the bottle down on the ground. They looked at each other.

"Okay. Together," said Jack. "One, two, three . . ."

"Turn us into Saint Bernard dogs!" they shouted into the cold wind.

Nothing happened.

Then suddenly, Jack was hurled face-first into

the snow. The world went black, and Jack felt his body shaking uncontrollably.

When the shaking stopped, Jack opened his eyes. He wasn't dizzy. He wasn't scared or worried or tired. He felt enormously happy. He looked down at himself. He was covered with thick red and white fur. He had four furry legs with big paws.

Something moved behind Jack. He turned and saw a fluffy tail waving. He leapt toward it. The tail moved away! Jack realized the tail was *his*! Still, it was fun to try to catch it. He turned in a circle, around and around and around.

Jack noticed fat snowflakes floating like feathers through the air. He stopped chasing his tail and bounced around clumsily, trying to eat the swirling flakes. He snapped at the air, until he heard another dog barking.

Jack understood the dog's language right away: "JACK! JACK!"

Jack looked at the Saint Bernard running

toward him through the snow. She was a little smaller, with smoother fur and bright, lively eyes. She barked, "WOW! WOW! CAN YOU BELIEVE THIS?"

Jack and Annie laughed with short bursts of loud panting. Their tongues hung out of their mouths, and their breath billowed into the cold. The world was alive with exciting sounds Jack had

never heard before. The sounds weren't loud, but they were clear and distinct.

Along with the *HEH-HEH-HEH!* of their heavy breathing, Jack heard the *swish-swish* of the wind-driven snow and the *crick-crack* of ice on the mountain slopes.

"SMELL!" barked Annie. She and Jack lifted their big black noses into the air and sniffed.

Strong scents wafted from all directions. Jack stepped forward, sniffing this way and that, his nostrils quivering. The smells changed with every step and every turn of his head. The sky had a scent. The distant chimney smoke, craggy rocks, and mountain slopes—all had different scents.

Jack smushed his nose into the newly fallen snow. The snow held a dozen different smells, all wonderful and amazing. Jack licked the snow like ice cream. It was so cold, it felt hot!

"JACK! JACK!" Annie barked again.

Jack looked up at her, his nose covered with snow.

Annie stood perfectly still, her paw up. Jack sniffed the air. The wind now carried different smells that stood out from all the others: a whiff of fish and crackers mixed with wet fur.

Amid the sounds of wind and ice, Jack heard distant barking.

"BARRY!" Jack barked. He had been so busy discovering what it was like to be a dog, he'd almost forgotten Barry!

Jack and Annie started yapping and bumping against each other. They bolted into the wind and the flying snow, scrambling over rocks and plowing through snowdrifts. Jack's four legs were nimble and strong. The freezing cold didn't bother him at all. He didn't feel a bit stiff. None of his muscles ached.

Jack and Annie ran this way and that, through the fresh mountain air, following sound and scent. As Barry's barking grew louder, they slowed down.

And then they saw him!

"BARRY!" Jack barked.

Barry stood on a small ridge above them, his tail high in the air. When he saw Jack and Annie, he looked surprised. He sniffed the air. He cocked his head to the side.

"IT'S US!" barked Annie.

Barry began yelping with glee. He leapt off the ridge, half tumbling, half running down the slope to greet them.

Barry's giant head pushed against Jack and

Annie. His eyes shone in the snowy afternoon light. As they all nudged each other and sniffed, three tails wagged in the air. Barry yowled and whined, "YOU'RE DOGS! HOW? HOW?"

"MAGIC!" barked Annie.

Barry sneezed, "OH! OKAY!" Then he went down on his front paws and barked, "LET'S PLAY!" The three of them started play fighting. They stood on their back legs and pushed each other around. Jack nipped at Barry's fur. Annie nibbled his ears.

Jack, Annie, and Barry bounced and barked and fell and fought, until finally they all collapsed into the snow and rolled over onto their backs, sticking their paws in the air.

Rubbing his furry back against the crunchy snow felt wonderful to Jack. He wiggled and rocked from side to side. Then he and Annie and Barry stood up and gave their wet bodies good shakes. They shook their heads, too, flinging drool and snow on each other.

But Jack didn't mind drool a bit now. He was

completely happy to be a big, furry dog playing in a snowstorm in the mountains. Even though the wind whipped against him and it was hard to see, he felt no fear. He was warm, his body was sturdy and strong, and he could smell and hear a whole new world of scents and sounds.

Relaxed and happy, Jack decided to give Barry some advice: "LISTEN, MAN," he barked, "IF YOU WANT TO STAY WITH THE MONKS, YOU HAVE TO GET SERIOUS AND ACT RESPONSIBLE!"

Barry turned his giant head from side to side, listening to Jack.

Jack barked: "DO NOT KNOCK PEOPLE OVER, AND WHEN THEY SAY, *SIT*, YOU SIT! SAME WITH *COME* AND *STAY*."

Barry looked curious. "HUH!" he barked.

"DON'T CHEW THINGS LIKE BOOKS," Jack barked. "AND DON'T CRY LIKE A PUPPY WHEN PEOPLE LEAVE YOU. YOU'RE A BIG, FUNNY DOG. BUT YOU COULD BE A *GREAT* DOG!"

Before Barry could answer, Jack felt a distant tremor, and he heard a *whumph!* He knew that sound! He sprang to his feet and lifted a paw, listening. Annie and Barry scrambled to their feet and listened, too.

Jack heard the sounds of rumbling and ice cracking and snow sliding.

Barry barked and bolted in the direction of the noises. Jack and Annie followed him down the pass. The three of them swerved around rocks and threaded their way along a narrow path. Then they stopped and whimpered and whined.

A pile of avalanche snow blocked their way. With barely a pause, Barry barreled on, his paws and powerful chest plowing through the snow, clearing a passage.

Jack and Annie plowed after Barry. Then they all stopped. A black hat was lying on top of the snow ahead of them! A knapsack with buckles lay next to it!

Barry, Jack, and Annie yelped and quivered

as they sniffed the hat and the knapsack. Jack smelled wool, metal, and leather.

"DIG! DIG!" Barry barked.

Jack, Annie, and Barry swiped at the snow with their huge paws. Bucketfuls of snow flew behind them. Whimpering and whining, they dug deeper and deeper. The more snow they cleared, the more smells Jack inhaled—hair, wool, blood.

Barry yelped. He had uncovered a face: a young man's face with brown hair matted against white skin, with bloody scratches and bluish lips. Jack remembered being caught in the avalanche and how the dogs had saved him. He barked at Barry, telling him to lick the man's face.

Barry swiped his warm tongue across the man's eyes and nose and mouth. Barry snuffled and whined and kept licking. He frantically licked the man's ears and hair.

Jack and Annie stood back, watching Barry work to save the avalanche victim. Barry's Saint Bernard instincts had taken over. He kept licking

and licking, until the man's eyelids fluttered open. The man blinked. Then he blinked again. He was alive! He tried to speak, but no sound came from his mouth.

Then something else seemed to grab Barry's attention. The dog jumped up and held his nose in the air. He barked, "STAY!" to Jack and Annie. "I'LL BE BACK! DIG!" Then he scrambled down the snowy passage and disappeared.

"BARRY!" Annie barked. She started to go after him.

"HE TOLD US TO STAY!" Jack barked. "KEEP DIGGING!"

Jack and Annie dug deeper and deeper into the snow. They uncovered the rest of the man's body—his blue, white, and red uniform with brass buttons, and his leather boots. They began licking his hands. They licked and licked until his fingers trembled. Jack and Annie barked with joy.

Suddenly Jack felt a shock pass through his body. It shot through his head, chest, back, and four legs. He and Annie were hurled away from the man in the snow. The world went black, and Jack felt his whole body shaking wildly.

Finally Jack was still. He opened his eyes. In a daze, he saw the French soldier lying in the snow nearby. Jack wasn't a Saint Bernard anymore. He was a person again.

Annie was a person, too. "I guess the magic hour just ended," she said.

CHAPTER NINE

Lovers of Knowledge

Jack and Annie crawled over to the soldier lying in the snow. "Hi there," said Annie, gently shaking him.

The young man opened his eyes. "Who are you?" he asked in a hoarse voice. "Where are the dogs?"

"The dogs are gone. We're Jack and Annie," said Annie. "We won't leave you."

"Thank you," breathed the young soldier, and he closed his eyes again. He was trembling with cold.

Annie pulled off her monk's robe and tucked it around the soldier. Jack did the same. Annie began rubbing one of the soldier's shaking hands, and Jack rubbed the other.

As the snow flew around them, Jack wondered what to do. Where was Barry? How could they get the soldier up on his feet? How would they find their way back to the monastery?

"Listen," said Annie, as if answering Jack's questions.

Jack heard distant voices. He heard booming barks. People were coming to help! And Barry was leading the way.

The huge dog bounded down the narrow passage to the young soldier. He seemed startled when he saw Jack and Annie. He sniffed them, and then barked his booming bark.

Jack wasn't sure what Barry was saying now. He wondered if it might be: "HOW THE HECK DID YOU CHANGE FROM DOGS BACK INTO PEOPLE?"

"Magic," Jack said.

Barry just panted, but Jack had the feeling he understood.

"Hello!" Brother Michael was hurrying up the narrow passage. Behind him were the two French soldiers who had stopped earlier at the monastery. The soldiers dropped to their knees and helped lift the avalanche victim to his feet. They wrapped Jack's and Annie's robes tightly around him.

"Did Barry find you?" Jack asked Brother Michael.

"Yes. We had just met these soldiers on the pass when Barry came running up to us," said the monk. "How did he get out of the monastery?"

"He escaped when we weren't looking," said Jack. "When we found him, he led us to the buried soldier."

"Amazing!" said Brother Michael.

Barry wagged his tail. It didn't seem to worry him any longer that Jack and Annie had turned back into people. *Dogs accept whatever comes along,* Jack thought.

"We must help this young man to the monastery," said Brother Michael. The two soldiers lifted the rescued man to his feet and helped him walk. "Barry, lead us home!"

Barry took the lead with Jack and Annie. The three soldiers and Brother Michael followed.

"I loved being a dog," Jack whispered to Annie. "I loved all of it. Didn't you? Didn't you love it?"

"Of course I did!" said Annie, grinning.

"Playing with you and Barry was one of the happiest things I've done in my life," said Jack. "And we helped teach him stuff, and we helped him save a life!"

"I know," said Annie.

As he hurried through the snow beside Barry, Jack tried to remember how it felt to be a dog. He moved quickly, keeping in step with Barry's prancing gait. He inhaled the cold, fresh wind, smelling woodsmoke and falling snow.

By the time they had all reached the monastery, the wind and snow had stopped. Jack held the door for Brother Michael and the three soldiers. Then he, Annie, and Barry followed them inside.

Father Laurent and another man were waiting for them in the torchlit hallway. The man wore a long gray overcoat and a large black hat in the shape of a triangle. He had a pale face, and his gray eyes were deeply set above a long, straight nose. Jack thought he looked familiar.

"So the missing officer has been found! Wonderful!" said Father Laurent. "Brother Michael, please make him comfortable by the fire in the parlor. Bring him some hot soup." Brother Michael led the soldiers down the hall.

"Jack and Annie," said Father Laurent, "may I present you to Consul Napoléon Bonaparte?"

Now Jack knew why the man looked so familiar! He had seen paintings of the famous military leader in history books.

Napoléon Bonaparte took off his hat and bowed his head. When he straightened up, he looked at Annie and Jack with a piercing gaze.

"Am I to understand you have saved my man from a snowy grave?" Napoléon Bonaparte said.

"Not us, Consul, sir," said Jack. "It was Barry."

The big dog was swinging his tail and panting.

"*Barry* saved the lost soldier?" exclaimed Father Laurent. "Oh, my! I knew that you were trying to train him. But I had no idea you could work miracles! How did you do it?"

"Well . . . I guess we know how to think like dogs," said Jack.

"Delightful! Good dogs! All three of you!" said Father Laurent, laughing.

Barry sneezed. Jack and Annie sneezed, too.

"I think we all need some hot tea and a fire," said Father Laurent. "Come. Let us go into my library."

"Thank you, but I fear I must be on my way," Napoléon Bonaparte said. "I will allow my three men to rest here, but I must return to camp. I will see you tomorrow with all your dogs. And of course"—he patted Barry's head—"I hope that this one leads the way. He is a great dog."

"Indeed he is," said Father Laurent. "Good afternoon, Your Excellency."

The French ruler opened the door and stepped out into the cold. He turned back and saluted them, then strode away alone through the snow.

Father Laurent closed the door. He looked at Jack and Annie and laughed. "This has been quite a day," he said, shaking his head. "I met Napoléon Bonaparte for the first time—and Barry became a true Saint! Let us celebrate with a cup of tea. A fresh pot is waiting in the library."

"Thank you, that sounds great," said Annie. She looked at Jack.

"Sure, cool," said Jack.

Jack, Annie, and Barry followed Father Laurent down the main hall. He opened the door to a large room lit with flickering candles and a blazing fire. Barry flopped down near the fireplace.

Jack and Annie looked around at the room. Shadows played on shelves with rows and rows of leather-bound books. Along one of the walls were glass cabinets filled with displays of butterflies, other insects, feathers, and rocks.

"Wow," breathed Jack. "This is a great room."

"I confess it is my favorite room in all the world," said Father Laurent. "I am a lover of knowledge."

"So are we," said Jack.

"Wonderful. I thought you might be," said the

monk. "Come, sit, please." He led them to a small table. They all sat down, and Father Laurent poured tea from a silver pot into three china cups.

As they each took a sip of the hot, sweet tea, Barry barked. He stood up and wagged his tail, staring at them. He barked again.

"He wants attention," said Father Laurent, shaking his head. "Quiet, Barry."

But Barry barked again.

"Oh!" said Annie. "I know what he wants! He wants to show you something! Barry, *stay*." She walked to the other side of the room. Barry didn't move.

"*Come*, Barry," said Annie.

Barry walked to Annie and stood very still.

"*Sit*, Barry," said Annie.

Barry sat. His tail thumped the stone floor.

"My! I can't believe it!" said Father Laurent. "It's like magic!"

"You have no idea," said Annie.

Jack laughed. "Good dog, Barry," he said.

"Perhaps you would like to brush him?" Father

Laurent said to Annie. The monk got a large brush from a shelf and gave it to her. "Brushing always makes a Saint happy, and Barry has more than earned his happiness today."

Annie got up from her chair and knelt beside Barry. As she gently brushed his beautiful, thick fur, Barry leaned against her and put his paw on her foot.

Father Laurent smiled. "A Saint leans against you to keep you warm," he said, "and he'll put his paw on your foot to keep it warm, too."

"You sound like you love dogs," said Annie.

"I do indeed," said Father Laurent. "I love all of nature. In fact, I often leave the monastery and go on expeditions just to study the natural world."

"What do you do on your expeditions?" asked Jack.

"Oh, I have gathered many rare specimens of butterflies, other insects, rocks, and minerals, as you can see from my displays," said Father Laurent, pointing to the cases in his library. "But I am a botanist first and foremost."

"A botanist?" said Annie.

"A botanist studies plants," said Father Laurent. He stood and walked over to a shelf and picked out a large book with a pale cloth cover. "*This* is my most precious treasure. On my mountain expeditions, I have found many rare and beautiful flowers. They are preserved in this book."

Jack's heart started to pound. "You mean you have *real* flowers in that book?" he asked.

"Yes," said Father Laurent. "Would you like to see them?"

Jack and Annie nodded.

Father Laurent smiled and brought the book over to the table.

CHAPTER TEN

Spirit of the Buttercup

Father Laurent sat down at the table and opened his book of flowers. Jack and Annie looked over the monk's shoulder. Even Barry stepped closer to the table and pushed his giant head under Father Laurent's elbow to look at the book.

The monk carefully turned the rough linen pages. The pages were blank, but pressed between them were leaves and flowers. Father Laurent gently held up a cluster of tiny pink flowers. The flowers were completely flat and dry, but they had kept all their petals and color.

"These are *Androsace alpina*. That's their scientific name. Their popular name is Alpine rock-jasmine," said the monk. "Several summers ago, I found these hidden among mountain rocks."

"Nice," said Annie.

Jack held his breath. *Could there be a white and yellow flower in the book?*

Father Laurent turned the page and very carefully picked up a dark golden flower. "This is *Caltha palustris*, better known as marsh marigold," he said. "I found this two years ago in the southern Alps."

"Lovely," said Annie.

Father Laurent turned the page again. He held up a dried white flower. "*Cerastium fontanum*, the mouse-ear chickweed," the monk said. "Its tiny petals look like the ears of a mouse."

"Cute," said Annie.

"Yes," said Father Laurent. He gently closed the cloth-covered book. "Since you like flowers so much, I assume you like butterflies, too. Let me show you my favorites." He started to stand up.

"No, wait, please," said Jack. He tried to keep his voice steady. "Do you happen to have a white and yellow flower in that book?"

Father Laurent frowned. "Hmm . . . let me see. Oh, yes, of course." He opened the book again and turned the pages until he found what he was looking for. He carefully held up a flower with white petals and a yellow center. It shone in the firelight, as if it were still alive.

"*Ranunculus glacialis*, the glacial butter-cup," said the monk. "One of the highest flowering plants in the Alps. A perfect specimen! I found it not far from our monastery just last summer."

"That's it," whispered Jack. "That's exactly what we're looking for!"

"You're looking for the glacial buttercup?" Father Laurent asked. "Why?"

"Why?" said Jack. He wasn't sure what to say.

"Uh, we have some friends who really love flowers," said Annie. "And when we were heading out to do our research in the Alps, they asked us to please try to find one of those and bring it back to them."

"I see," said the monk. "Well, then allow me to give you this glacial buttercup to take back to your friends. I'm sure I can find another later in the summer. It is the least I can do to thank you for the wonderful work you did with Barry today."

"Thank you!" said Jack.

"Do you know if the glacial buttercup has any special meaning?" said Annie.

Father Laurent squinted at the flower. "Well, throughout history many flowers have had special meanings," he said. "Let me think."

"Wait, please," said Jack. He quickly pulled out his notebook and pencil. "Okay. Ready."

"If I recall, buttercups stand for childhood, the carefree, open spirit of childhood," said Father Laurent. "Such a joyful spirit can brighten even the most bleak and barren places."

Jack quickly wrote:

> Buttercups:
> Spirit of childhood
> Joyful, carefree, open

Jack looked at Father Laurent. "That sounds like the spirit of a dog," he said. He stroked Barry's ear. It felt like warm velvet.

Father Laurent smiled. "Yes. Yes, it does," he said. "Dogs and children share a common spirit. I do agree with that."

Jack and Annie looked at each other. "Well,

I guess we'd better leave now," said Jack. He put away his pencil and notebook.

"Can you not stay another night?" asked Father Laurent. "It will be dark soon."

"That's okay. We can find our way home, even in the dark," said Jack.

"And where is home?" asked the monk.

"Oh . . . it's down the mountain a ways," said Annie. "It's not exactly in the first village you come to, but just outside that village, you know, before you see the church steeple. There you turn left onto a winding path and then go awhile, and then turn right—and then left . . ." She shrugged. "Well, we know how to find it."

"I see," said Father Laurent, though he looked a little bewildered. He stood up. "Let's carefully pack your flower, so you can carry it to your friends." The monk took two pieces of thick paper from the flower book and placed the glacial buttercup between them. Then he handed it to Jack.

Jack gently placed the flower at the bottom of his bag. Then Father Laurent led Jack and Annie out of the library.

Barry followed them down the hallway. When they reached the front hall, Annie looked at the big dog. "You have to stay here, Barry," she said.

Barry's tail stopped wagging.

"Perhaps he can walk with you part of the way," said Father Laurent. "Then just send him back to me. I think now that you've trained him, he can come back home by himself."

"Great, thank you!" said Annie.

Father Laurent opened the front door. "Farewell, my friends. Travel safely," he said. "Come back for dinner, Barry."

Barry barked as if he understood and then bounded out into the snow. Jack and Annie followed him. The snow had completely stopped, and the sky was clear. The setting sun cast a brilliant light over the mountains.

Jack remembered that the tree house had

landed on a slope above the wide pass. His sense of direction seemed keener than before. "I think we originally came from *that* way," he said. "Let's try it."

Jack led Annie and Barry away from the monastery. His eyes searched the pass for signs of the tree house, until finally he thought he saw it: brown wood nestled on a slope among gray boulders. "That's it!" he said, pointing. "Over there!"

Jack started to run, and Annie and Barry ran with him. As they raced through the clean, crisp air, Jack remembered what it felt like to be a dog. The cold didn't bother him at all; he didn't feel sore or stiff. Nothing hindered his body. And most of all, he felt a wild joy. He felt as if he could run forever.

Finally, laughing and panting, Jack, Annie, and Barry reached the base of the slope below the tree house. The setting sun covered the mountaintops with purple light.

Barry barked. Jack could tell he wanted to climb into the tree house with them. "You have to go back to Father Laurent now, Barry," Jack said softly. He tugged on Barry's velvety ear. "But we think you're a *great* dog, and so does Napoléon."

Barry made a snuffling sound. Annie turned her face away from Barry and Jack.

"Annie, aren't you going to say good-bye to him?" said Jack.

Annie looked at Jack. Her eyes were filled with tears. "How do I do that?" she said. "How do I say good-bye to him?"

"You tell him how you feel about him. Tell him about all the good things waiting for him back at the monastery," said Jack. "The fire, the food, Father Laurent and Brother Michael, and all the other dogs. You tell him he's going to save lots of lives."

Annie knelt down and put her arms around Barry's giant head. He licked her as she clutched him.

"Tell him, Annie," Jack urged her.

Annie lifted Barry's ear and whispered into it for a long time. Jack couldn't hear all that she said, but he caught the words *love* and *all my life.*

Then Annie stood up and pointed toward the monastery. Smoke was rising from the chimney. "Go home now, Barry," she said. "It's where you belong."

Barry looked from Annie to Jack. He sneezed. Then he climbed down the slope and took off for home.

Annie turned away quickly and wiped her eyes. "Let's go," she said, and she scrambled up the slope and climbed through the tree house window.

Jack followed her. Inside the tree house, he picked up the Pennsylvania book and pointed to a picture of the Frog Creek woods. "I wish we could go home, where *we* belong," he said.

Booming dog barks came from the distance. Echoes of the barks filled the air. Barking echoed from all directions—the sky, the clouds, the rocky slopes, and the purple mountain peaks of the Great St. Bernard Pass.

Then the wind began to blow.

The tree house started to spin.

It spun faster and faster.

Then everything was still.

Absolutely still.

❊ ❊ ❊

Jack and Annie were wearing their jeans and sweatshirts again. Jack's bag was a backpack. No time at all had passed in Frog Creek. Dawn was still breaking. Dogs were barking in the distance, and the woods were filled with birdsong.

"You okay?" Jack asked Annie.

She nodded.

"Barry's going to save lots of lives," said Jack. "I know it."

Annie smiled. "He was so funny," she said wistfully.

"Yeah, and he was happy," said Jack. He reached into his backpack and carefully lifted out the papers with the glacial buttercup. He handed the dried flower to Annie, then pulled out their rhyme and reread it:

> *The second thing to break the spell*
> *is a white and yellow flower.*
> *Live its meaning for yourself,*
> *if only for an hour.*

"I guess we did live its meaning for an hour," said Jack.

"That joyful spirit that Father Laurent talked about?" said Annie.

Jack nodded. "For exactly an hour, while I was a dog, I was perfectly happy," he said.

"Only for an hour, perfectly happy?" said Annie.

Jack shrugged. "The rest of the time, I was pretty worried."

"About what?" said Annie.

"Well, in the beginning, of course, I worried about the avalanche and losing you," said Jack. "Then I worried that Teddy and Kathleen had sent us to the wrong place. I worried about finding the flower. I worried about wasting time training Barry. Then I worried about finding him."

"You worry a lot, Jack," said Annie.

"I know," said Jack. "I needed a dog to teach me how to have a child's joyful spirit."

"And Barry needed *you* to learn how to be responsible," said Annie. "You taught him how to listen to others and how to find avalanche victims. You helped bring out Barry's instincts to be a rescue dog, Jack. You did a great job."

"Oh . . ." Jack felt his face getting red. "Well, you did a great job, too. You really did."

"Whatever," Annie said modestly. "At least we found the second thing to help save Penny." She carefully placed the glacial buttercup in the corner of the tree house.

Jack reached into his bag, took out the emerald rose, and placed it beside the flower.

"We have two things so far," said Annie.

"And two more to go," said Jack.

"But right now, we have to hurry home and sneak back into our rooms and put on our pajamas and get into our beds, so Mom and Dad can wake us up and tell us to get ready for school," said Annie.

Jack laughed. "We live a weird life," he said.

"Yep," said Annie, "but I like it all."

"Me too," said Jack. And they started down the rope ladder, headed for home.

Author's Note

For me, the joy of writing the Magic Tree House books is discovering different facts and then putting them together with my imagination to create a story. When I was doing research on the Saint Bernard Monastery in the Swiss Alps, I discovered three things:

• Laurent Murith (known as Father Laurent) was the head of the monastery in 1800. He was also a great botanist and naturalist. The library of the monastery held many of his specimens, including the linen book with the pressed flowers.

• With help from Father Laurent and from the dogs and monks of the monastery, First Consul Napoléon Bonaparte crossed the Alps in 1800 with sixty thousand soldiers. Remarkably, not one man died on the grueling trek.

• In 1800, a young Saint Bernard dog named Barry lived at the monastery. Barry saved more than forty lives between 1800 and 1812. He was considered the most heroic dog of all time in the Alps. After his death, the monks always named one of their dogs Barry.

Another great joy for me in writing these books is learning a lot more about subjects I love. And I don't think there is any subject I love more in this world than dogs—especially dog heroes. To learn more about the incredible dogs of the Saint Bernard Monastery and other heroic dogs, you can read *Dog Heroes* (the companion nonfiction book to *Dogs in the Dead of Night*), which I have cowritten with my sister, Natalie Pope Boyce.

Dogs in the Dead of Night

In the past, the nonfiction Magic Tree House books were called Research Guides. Now we've changed the name to Fact Trackers. Why? Because my sister and I always feel like· we're "tracking the facts" as we write about a new topic. The Magic Tree House Fact Trackers are for kids like you (and me!) who want to know more facts than I can fit into a story. If you haven't fact-tracked with Jack and Annie yet, you are in for a new kind of adventure!

Mary Pope Osborne

Track the facts about dog heroes with Jack and Annie!

Coming December 2011

Don't miss Magic Tree House® #47
(A Merlin Mission)

Abe Lincoln at Last!

Jack and Annie have to help one of the most famous presidents of all!